Beyond Time

Beyond Time

Poems from North of the Tension Line

Larry Christianson

For Diane Segner Pauls—
Larry Christianson

NORTH STAR PRESS OF ST. CLOUD, INC.
St. Cloud, Minnesota

Cover art by Norma Christianson
Author photo by Norma Christianson

Copyright © 2008 Larry Christianson

All rights reserved.

ISBN-10: 0-87839-292-0
ISBN-13: 978-0-87839-292-6

Printed in the United States of America

First Edition: July 2008

Published by
North Star Press of St. Cloud, Inc.
P.O. Box 451
St. Cloud, Minnesota 56302

northstarpress.com

info@northstarpress.com

Dedicated

to
Norma Christianson and Tom Plihal—
very special and longtime traveling companions on journeys
north of the tension line. May the adventures continue!

List of Illustrations

Detail of "At Lake Three" by Norma Christianson 1

Detail of "At Lake Three" by Norma Chistianson 13

"Root Beer Falls" by Tom Plihal 20

"Early Morning on the Water at Horse Lake" by Tom Plihal 46

"Moon Set" by Norma Christianson 51

"Lone Maple" by Tom Plihal 55

"Misty Morning Moose" by Tom Plihal 57

Contents

Beyond Time xi

Up North Reflections

Up North Reflections 3
Sands of Life 4
Moments and Meanings 5
Jump Off 6
Yooperland 7
Endless Day 8
Spirit Footprints 9
Northland Nightfall 10
Healing Streams 11

Boundary Waters

Wilderness Traces 15
Island Mist 16
Bear Camp 17
Tough Carry 18
Portage Connection 19
Root Beer Falls 21
Shell Lake 22
Biffy View 23
La Croix Landing 24
End of the Road 25
Paddle Inn 26
Brittons Cafe 27
Berried Treasures 28
Solo by Sixty 29
Under Cover 30
Chainsaw Sisters 31
Buzz Brothers 32
Long John Blue 33
Snow Camp 34

Run Silent 35
Simple Truth 36
Sunnies 37
Moose Maple 38
Wind Lake 39
Carp Falls 40
Misty Morning Moose 41
Endless River 42
Suffer City 43
Beer Keg Pond 44
Wind Bound 45
In the Cedars 47
Rainy Day 48
Double Eagle 49
Moon Set 50
Tomorrow River 52
Golden October 53
Lone Maple 54
Isle of Dreams 56

North of the Tension Line

North of the Tension Line 59
Places of the Heart 60
Diamond Hour 61
Blue Shadows 62
Lonely Loons 63
Endless Rocks 64
Steam Rising 65
Soul Whispers 66
Soul Wrinkles 67

BEYOND TIME

Horse Lake—
Place beyond time
    where motion is measured
        by sun traveling
            through sky,
        by water rippling
           over rock,
              ancient and scattered
                  everywhere.

Time transcended by place
    where beauty is defined
        by forest teeming
           with life
           and death,
        by moon shining
           on lake,
              calm and moving
                  nowhere.

Horse Lake—
    where time stands still,
    where place blends naturally
        with serenity.

—August 2004 while at Horse Lake in the Boundary Waters Canoe Area Wilderness

Up North Reflections

UP NORTH REFLECTIONS

Up North Reflections—
Tumbling down through the years
    woven into folksy patterns
        down to earth and near to heart.
Places and spaces.
Beneath and beyond
    compass point—N.
Pointing toward old dreams
    and new adventures,
        and deep longings of the spirit.

Up North—
A universal metaphor
    transcending all maps
        and compass headings.
A very special place
    dwelling within minds
        and inspiring hearts.
A vast space as varied
    as the inner landscape
        of humanity.

Up North—
A treasured retreat
    of vague definition or precise location.
For meaningful memories
    along magic pathways
        of renewal.
For changes of pace
    and cherished getaways
        from rising responsibilities
            of life at home.
Beyond and beneath geography—
    reflections in all directions
        north.

—June 2007 for poetry reading at the Mocha Monkey Coffee Shop in Waconia

SANDS OF LIFE

Motion.
Endless motion . . .

The movement dances
        upon swirling waters
                of life.

Turning,
       twirling,
       twisting,
             turning,
      always turning . . .

The reality of change
      presses on
      in relentless
             movements.

Motion.
Endless motion . . .

The pulsating waves roll on,
        pounding shorelines,
        churning sands of life
             upside down.

—May 1980 an old favorite voicing expression to the reality of change

MOMENTS AND MEANINGS

Moments
    come and go—
        quickly,
        relentlessly.
Time passing on
    in a flash—
    moving into more time,
        more experiences,
        more happenings.
More moments
    blending into memory,
    inviting the making
        of meaning.

Meanings
    emerge and endure—
        slowly,
        patiently.
Connections taking shape
    in changing realities—
    moving into more connections,
        more opportunities,
        more relationships.
More meanings
    enriching memory,
    encouraging the cherishing
        of moments.

—July 2005 reflections while camped at Horse Lake

JUMP OFF

Jump off.
Place of adventure
    for all journeys
    into wild territory –
      within.
And on a map.
Strategic starting points
    for expeditions
    of wondering hearts
      and wandering spirits.

Jump off.
Place of beginnings
    and beginning anew—
      fresh perspectives,
      adventurous attitudes,
      challenging experiences,
      open horizons,
      high hopes
        and lofty dreams.

Unknown country
    of heightened awareness
    and sharper focus.
Like a gentle whisper
    of intrigue
    and hints
      of romance.
Flowing free
    on fresh breezes
    of every jump off
      dawning,
      unfolding
In great anticipation.

—July 2007 for all beginning times

YOOPERLAND

End of the line
    up state,
        downtrodden
            tired territory.
Landscape of desertion
    sweeping across forgotten outposts
    of past glories
        long gone.

Mom and Popville
    abandoned gradually
    for fast food paradise
        and chain lodging,
    for empty parking lots
        and faded dreams.
Even old churches
    appearing desolate
    like museum relics
        left behind carelessly.
Not unlike fields of flowers
    trampled by castaway cars,
    rusting home appliances,
    and broken down toilets
        littering among weeds
        blooming.
Beautiful in a quirky
    north woods way
    with pine scent mingling
        in paper mill poison.

Sparkling waters
    and stone outcroppings
    define a rugged Yooperland
        along with ceramic deer,
        and carved bears
Outnumbering people.

—June 2006 rolling along on US 2 in Upper Michigan

ENDLESS DAY

Lightness
   hanging on
   in many shades
       and nuances
       of color.

Fading slowly
   into an endless twilight
   of never really dark,
       always light
       in the sky.

Lightness
   slipping away
   into dancing shadows
       of sunrise
       and sunset.

Blending peacefully
   into endless day.

—*July 2003 in Oslo, Norway, in fascination of long summer days at sixty degrees north lattitude*

SPIRIT FOOTPRINTS

Spirit footprints
  dance lightly,
      hopefully.

Across hearts
  imprinted with echoes
      of old memories
      awakening,
  etched forever
      in new visions
      dawning.

In the Springtime
  of creation splendor
      bursting forth
      in beauty.

—March 2007 with Springtime renewal vision hopefully in sight

NORTHLAND NIGHTFALL

Northland
Nightfall
   spreads slowly
     across landscapes
         yearning.

For calm.
For slumber
  as daylight
    surrenders to darkness
        arriving.

Tumbling
Through twilight.

—November 2007 in appreciation of evening quiet and peacefulness

HEALING STREAMS

Stories.
Always stories.
Converge and diverge
    like old stones
        concealed beneath
            a river.

Gently moving.
Fast flowing.
Merging with currents
    invisible,
    yet strong.

Disguised
    in innocence
    by dancing diamonds
        of sunlight.
Sparkling
    on the surface
    of darkness.
Hiding sharp edges
    of sorrow.

Grinding together
    like old stones,
    smooth
    in the healing streams
        of time.

—February 2007 from the healing mystery of stones and streams

Boundary Waters

WILDERNESS TRACES

Leave no trace
   on wilderness landscapes.

Traces remain—
   etched on my heart
      forever free.
And spirit soaring.
Transcending passages
   of time and place.
Sparking imagination.
Kindling renewal
   in canoe country
      up north.
Return often—
   cherished memories
      of trips past.
And new adventures.
Looming on open horizons
   of dreams unfolding.

Turning into wilderness
   traces.

—August 2007 for inscription of canoe journal of all my trips in the Boundary Waters over the years

ISLAND MIST

Reflections.
Shimmering in morning
    sunshine—
        golden on wings
            of dayglow.

Ancient granite boulders.
Brooding in pine forest
    shadows—
        gray on shorelines
Emerging from misty
    island stillness.

Solitude.
Seeping through waters
    calm—
        peaceful in shades
            of blue.
Penetrating restless hearts
    with serenity
        in misty island
            retreat.

—September 2007 with meaningful memories of many misty mornings in the boundary waters

BEAR CAMP

Long ago
Yet always near
    in memory,
    in moments
        of wilderness camping.

And thinking about bears.

Ensign Lake nightmare
    of fear and trembling
    and food lost,
        along with innocence.
Hungry bear
    arriving along shoreline,
    low and pebbly,
        grinding in the darkness
            of night.

All night.
Time after time
    punching and pounding,
    pulling our fragile food pack
        down from not so lofty
            limb.

In bear camp.

—August 2006 while in the Boundary Waters thinking of bears and my brother Al and Ensign Lake way back in 1980

TOUGH CARRY

Tough carry
      in wilderness
           wonder.

Folbot
      through forest
         folly.
A novice blunder.
Mighty struggle
    all the way
      to Shell Lake
        and back.
A miracle
      to keep on paddling
         and portaging.

For years to come!

—*August 2007 with thoughts of carrying the old canvas covered Folbot on the Shell portage back in 1975*

PORTAGE CONNECTION

The portage trail looms
    ahead in the distance.
Narrow passageway
    from one lake
        to another.
Guarded by huge pines
    and rocky outcrops
    of the Canadian Shield.

A necessary portion of the journey.
Connecting link
    from present situation
        to future location.
Portage difficulty,
    a struggle with all effort,
    eyes and thoughts
    focused on the end:
        shimmering water,
        refreshing breeze,
        paddle in hand,
        canoe gliding.

Portage connection—
    to be endured
        or enjoyed?
    to experience not as burden
        but as treasure!

—August 1980 portage realities from very early in our wilderness traveling

ROOT BEER FALLS

Root Beer Falls
  on Sioux River
  flowing north
      in wilderness splendor.
Calm passage
  through murky muskeg
  and bending stalks
      of wild rice.
All the way to Elm Portage
  descending elevation
  in rushing rapids.
Cascading water.
Crashing through tumbling timber
  and glistening boulders
      of river bed
      shifting—
  always shifting
  in timeless rhythm
      of the north country.
Plunging over granite
  ancient
  and free.
Bronze foam
  rich in color,
  smooth in texture,
  turbulent in motion.
Flashing rainbow hues
  in dim afternoon
      sunlight.
Slanting through pine treetops.
Reflecting unchanging reality
  in the always changing
      landscape
      of Root Beer Falls.

—September 2004 on the way to Shell Lake with friend Tom in a high-water autumn

SHELL LAKE

Sparkling waters.
Brooding islands.
Shining like diamonds—
  a precious treasure
  glowing in the sinking
     sun.

Shell Lake.
Canoeing companions.
Weaving memories
  through three decades
  of camping
  along shores
     wildly free.

Of time and place.
Of rock and forest.
Of sky and lake.
Only passing through—
  briefly,
  respectfully.

Leaving no trace.

—September 2004 on one of many canoe trips into Shell Lake

BIFFY VIEW

Natural rhythms
    moving
    in open air.

Beautiful forest vista
    growing
    in summer sweetness.
Wilderness biffy view—
    fresh pine boughs,
    tiny trillium blooming
        in shades of white,
    blueberry bushes
        hugging the ground,
        not yet ripe for picking,
    sparkling water
        rolling on gentle breezes
        toward distant shores.

Natural rhythms
    contemplating
    in peaceful wonder.

—July 2000 from the biffy at the southeast bay campsite on Shell Lake

LA CROIX LANDING

Floats on the water.

Lac La Croix
    calm morning,
        cessna landing.
Splash down
    near Bottle Portage.
Spray flashing
    in sunlight
        shimmering.

Pilot Bud.
Friend Tom.
A canoe landing
    on the water.

Adventure begins—
    where control ends.

—September 2003 with Tom on our much talked about fly in and paddle out fall canoe trip

END OF THE ROAD

Heard
My old friend
   Bob—
Through
Green River Boys
   singing in gravel voice
   on the side porch
       in far north Ely.

At the end of the road:
   "Oowee ride me high.
    Oowee we gonna fly."
You ain't going nowhere
   not even slow
       much less fast.

In a glimpse
   of fleeting clarity
   and bumbling confusion,
   evoking fuzzy images
       of Ghengis Khan
       and his brother
          Don.
Mixed up metaphors
   of walking fish,
   a talking dog,
       and Gungadin.

Dylan—
   around the bend
   and back again,
       always again.
On the way somewhere
   past nowhere.

—*August 2006 from Tuesday evening music on the streets in Ely*

PADDLE INN

Paddle in
        through wilderness waters
            clear and calm,
    among ancient rocks
    framing boreal forests
        with rugged texture,
        and ragged perspective
            set against
            majestic skies.

Paddle Inn.
WELY—
    end of the road radio,
    transmitting timeless treasures
    throughout the north
        country.
Canoe Country Outfitters.

Paddle in
    to new found serenity
    and peaceful soothing
        of the spirit.
And paddle out
    to renewal.

—August 2006 for Dan and Rose in Ely with thanks for wonderful hospitality

BRITTONS CAFE

Brittons.
Newly remodeled
    and pretty much
    the same decor
        and food.

Smoke free café
    at the end
    of the road.
And around the bend
    of time changing
        and realities
Rearranging.
Even in north country
    Minnesota.

Brittons.
Boundary Waters
    beginning breakfast
    for countless canoe
        adventurers.
In many ways
    a long way
    from Montigue Street.
Tangled up
    in only blue sky
    and sparkling waters
        of serenity.

—July 2007 fueling up for canoeing with Bob Dylan on the radio at this down home Ely institution

BERRIED TREASURES

Bear patch
      picking,
       hunting.
For berried
      treasures.

Not a novelty
      tea creation
        at Chocolate Moose.
Nor a new
      ice cream flavor
        at Sherry's drive-in.

Searching
      for delicate,
        delicious,
          ripe and wild

Blueberries.

—July 2007 while in Ely staging out for a solo canoe trip

SOLO BY SIXTY

Long time longing.
Decades old dreaming—
    evolving,
    unfolding,
    emerging finally,
        partially,
            in hesitant reality.

Faltering through weakness
    into the light
        of new strength
        and resolve.

Solo by Sixty.

Alone in a lonely land.
Paddling through chapters
    of life story.
Portaging over pathways
    of difficult crossings—
        physical,
        emotional,
        vocational,
        spiritual.

Fishing away tension
    and troubles.
Camping atmosphere
    of calm relaxation.
Easing mind.
Warming heart.
Renewing spirit.
Refreshing body—
    able and aging
        gracefully.

—August 2005 on solo canoe trip at Tin Can Mike Lake

UNDER COVER

End of the road
   wilderness reality.
Rambling
Through north woods
   town—
Under cover of darkness,
        of deception.

Logging trucks
   loaded with timber
   fresh cut—
Rolling on the only route
   possible,
     clanging chains,
     chugging along
         quickly.

Though not quietly.
Long before dawn,
   like pirates—
Hauling forbidden treasure
   from precious forest
        preserves.

—August 2007 while in Ely overnight before a canoe trip

CHAINSAW SISTERS

Hilltop hideout
    between wilderness lakes—
        Pickett.
        Mudro.
Deep in north woods
    forest country.
Down six miles
    of gravel raodway
    off Echo Trail.
Old fashioned saloon
    overlooking muddy creek
    boundary waters entry.
Point of departure
and arrival—
        anticipation,
        culmination
            of adventure.

Antique chainsaws
    decorating the porch.
Autographed dollar bills
    plastered on the ceiling.
Goofy posters and pictures
    offering wisdom
    on the walls.
Basic beer—
    ice cold
    on the edge
        of civilization.
    Leinenkugel's Original.
    Grain Belt Premium.

Sisters guarding the gateway
    to wilderness
        and sanity.

—*September 2005 from solo canoe trip*

BUZZ BROTHERS

Buzz Brothers.
Buddies longing for adventure,
    waiting out steady rain
    and penetrating drizzle,
        and impatience—
    hanging out on a rustic,
            rambling
Old porch.

Littered with broken dreams
    and rusty chainsaws
    and a quirky collection
        of gaudy high heel shoes.

Wilderness visions
    chased by a bear in the biffy
    and ice cold Grain Belts
        in the old spirit
        of prairie suds.
Nestled deep in tall pines
    overlooking Pickett Lake
        and Mudro Creek.

Stenciled on burnt orange cloth.
Flaky humor
    and chainsaw sisters
        getting buzzed at the saloon,
            glowing grandly
            in the harvest moon.

—October 2005 for canoe guy friends Tom, Steve and Graham

LONG JOHN BLUE

At Shell portage.
Long John Blue—
    in full one piece
    suit of underwear.

Rising from middle
    of fully loaded
        canoe.
Shaking unsteady.
Surrounded by shotguns
    and fishing poles,
    and too many walleyes.
Plus companions
    with goofy grins
    and drunken smiles
        in autumn glory.

Plastic whiskey and soda
    bottles—
Clutched in each hand
    as the surly voice
    of Long John Blue
        boomed:
"Do you guys wanna drink?"

—August 2007 from a very real experience with friend Tom on the way to Shell Lake

SNOW CAMP

September.
On the water.
Friends helping friends
   on a troubled journey
   paddling downwind.

Past Isle of Dreams.
With an unwelcome plunge
   in chilly autumn
        nightmare.
Waking to howling winds
   and swirling snow
        squalls.
And freezing temperatures.
At Lake Three.

Friends drying clothes
   and mending spirits
   in the warmth
        of snow camp.

—*September 2007 with canoe friends Tom, Steve and Graham at Lake Three on a real Fall canoe trip adventure*

RUN SILENT

Run silent
   through wintry wilderness
      splendor.

Majestic pines laboring
  under heavy burdens
  of fresh snow
     clinging.
Ancient boulders brooding
  in morning stillness.
Shadows from sunshine bright,
  casting shades of gray,
     intriguing
        upon quiet shorelines.

North country solitude
  shattered
  by piercing yelps
     of huskie dogs
      straining restraints.
Wild barking frenzy,
  excitement rising,
  tension mounting—
     ready to run!!
More than ready
  to pull sled and musher
    into a burst
    of powder flying,
  strength in action,
  power in motion.

Run free.
Run silent
  in the thrilling spirit
    of adventure.

—*February 2001 for Norma's fiftieth birthday dog sledding adventure in the boundary waters*

SIMPLE TRUTH

Why do you
      suppose—

To propose.
The best place
      to fish
        is near camp!

Nearly always—
Not a long paddle
      across the lake.
Nor a bushwacking hike
      through the woods.
Not even a few portages
      over yonder.

Oh how I
      wonder—

Why it took so long
      to finally learn
        a simple truth.

—July 2007 on a simple truth that took me a long time to wrap my mind around

SUNNIES

Sunnies—
After all
   the windswept trolling
   and chasing game fish
      through years
      of canoe paddling.

And fishing.
Monster northern pike,
Feisty smallmouth bass,
   and illusive walleyes
   in wilderness waters
      inviting.

A graduation to panfish—
   to tiny waxie worms
      and ultra light
      rod and reel,
   to backwater bays
      and calm,
      weedy coves,
   to lots of fun.

And great eating
   every time—
      guaranteed!

—*July 2007 on finally discovering the joy of panfish in the Boundary Waters on my thirty-ninth canoe trip*

MOOSE MAPLE

Moose maple.
Downsized,
   as shrub browse.
Hugging fragile shorelines
   and protected hillsides.
Sheltered in shadows
   of massive boulders
   and old growth pines.

Moose maple.
Blazing bright
   in flame red
   and burnt orange.
Against forest background
   of birch yellow,
        aspen gold
        and evergreens.

Towering in October sunshine.
Standing noble guard
   over a changing
        panorama
        of beauty.

—October 2007 with friend Tom at Wind Lake in boundary waters autumn

WIND LAKE

Wilderness
        in late autumn
                array—
Golden hillsides
        stretching uphill
        all the way
                to Wind Lake.
Relaxing
        in cold wind
                howling,
                blowing.

Beware.
Take care.
Wind on the water.

Moving relentlessly
        across rocky points.
Crashing wildly
        into sandy shorelines.
Swirling hopefully
        around rugged islands.

Calm in the lee.
Peace before the storm
        arriving.

—October 2007 on my last canoe trip before turning sixty

CARP FALLS

Flashing golden
   in deep, dark
   rushing waters
      below Carp Falls.

Knife River
   brooding,
   tumbling,
   twisting along border
      route.
Offering paddlers
   a landscape of solitude
      and beauty
         beyond boundaries.

Artificial.
International.
Sensational
   in the catching
   of a magnificent carp
      at Carp Falls.

All the while wearing
   an old,
   tattered
   "Club Carp" tee shirt.

—*July 2007 from years ago on the Knife River*

MISTY MORNING MOOSE

Surprise—
    at dawn rising.
      Misty morning moose
        chasing,
        splashing,
        swimming in the heat
            of autumn ritual.

Out of heavy fog
    shrouding vision,
    haunting sounds
        of ancient longings.

Over on pine island,
    cow and bull—
    crashing through trees
        and underbrush,
    slipping on rocks,
    grunting in pursuit
        of annual fancies.

Moose—
    in water chilly.
    Chasing dreams
        and desires
        and one another!

—*November 2000 from a spectacular Fall canoe trip experience with Tom at Lake Four*

ENDLESS RIVER

Partners in the voyage.
Paddling north
    on endless river –
        meandering,
           winding around bends
                too many to count.

Flowing slowly,
    steadily along through fields
        of wild rice
           teeming with autumn's
                black harvest,
past beaten down moose runs
        and shoreline swamp grasses
            waving in the breeze.

Endless River.
Ending in a numbing
    completeness.

—*September 2006 reflections on Tom's description of paddling the Little Indian Sioux River*

SUFFER CITY

Suffer city—
Wilderness style.

Stretching across twenty five years
      and spanning
      a generation of aging
           and adventures.
Not getting any easier
      as aching muscles
      and dreaming hearts
      still paddle and portage.

Our favorite wilderness route
      to Shell Lake:
      Little Indian Sioux River
          through Elm Portage
          to Upper Pauness Lake.
      Around the awesome horseshoe
      beaver dam.
      All the way to Shell
          via a long carry
          through the woods
          into the place of magic
              in our memories
              and experiences.
Splendor and beauty
      aging gracefully
      through timeless centuries
          of evolution.

Suffer city—
As the land endures
      and thrives.

—*July 2000 at Shell Lake on our first canoe trip of the twenty-first century*

BEER KEG POND

Waiting.
Patiently
    with fishing poles ready
    on the little pond
        between Lakes
        One and Two.

Cruising shoreline weedbeds.
Waiting to portage
    sensibly
    with happy hour
        happening,
        consuming the group
Of eight burly guys
    clogging the portage,
    and drawing down
        a beer keg.

Toasting boisterously
    a sudsy completion
    of a wild time
        in the wilderness.

—July 2007 while waiting out a portage party

WIND BOUND

Unseen energy
    and mounting motion.
Rising on water,
    slowly—
        then gathering momentum
            and strength
                beyond a whisper.
High in the red pines.

Wind—
    howling from the south,
    blowing up a gale
        on Horse Lake,
    offering a wise warning
        to all who paddle:
            beware!

Be wary as whitecaps roll
    and surging waves
        pound ancient shoreline rocks
        with fury.
Be weary as gusts whip through camp,
    battering relentlessly
        all who seek refuge
            and calm,
    ravaging mercilessly
        campers wind bound
        in the safety
            of the company
            of one another.

—August 2006 at Horse Lake island campsite in the Boundary Waters Canoe Area

IN THE CEDARS

Campsite
    in the cedars.
        Rugged trees—
            old and gnarled
                through wilderness
                      weather extremes.

Canopy of shade
    and serenity.
        Ragged shoreline—
            new and eroded
                through wave and wind
                      action.

Peaceful days.
Rainy nights.
Together
    in the cedars.

—*July 2005 at Horse Lake with Norma*

RAINY DAY

Rainy day
Hanging out
    at the campsite.

Settling in
    to an even slower,
        calmer pace.
Enjoying smells
    of pine freshness,
    sounds of droplets,
        gently,
    as water cleanses
        the land.
New life opportunities
    in abundance
        thankfully.

And fear not—
Rain always stops!

—August 2006 at Horse Lake enjoying rain

DOUBLE EAGLE

Bald eagle.
Basking in morning glow
    on the high edge
    of rising rays
        of sunshine.
Golden warmth
    reflecting in calm waters
    of a little bay
        on Lake Three.

Bald eagle.
Watching from red pine crown
    in majestic loneliness,
    like a stately royal
        guarding the kingdom.

From aloft.
Aloof to our presence
    in the wilderness.
And our inspiration
    of double eagle image
    against a beautiful
        north country canvas
        of sky blue waters.

—July 2007 with Norma at island campsite on Lake Three

MOON SET

    Moon set
        sinking slowly,
        reflecting fully
                in Lake Three.

    Still water morning—
        awakening,
        dawning in blue haze
            unfolding,
            bending.

    In slow motion
        solitude,
        peacefulness
                brightening gradually.
    Into forest background
        from midnight black
        to lush green splendor
                teeming with life.

    Along waters lapping—
        gently,
        calmly
        on silent rocks
                speaking.
    In ancient voices
        soothing.

—March 2008 to accompany Norma's photo from Lake Three in summer 2007

TOMORROW RIVER

Tomorrow River.
Running swiftly
   through sorrow soothing,
      pain healing
       as water gently
          flows—

Winding slowly
  along memory banks,
     landmark moments
     of yesterday—

Merging streams
 of meaning
 all along
    the boundary
    of today.

—November 2006 while waiting at Abbott Northwestern Hospital in Minneapolis

GOLDEN OCTOBER

Golden October.
Autumn splendor
    on the water
    on the boundary
        of solitude
            growing within my heart
                of healing.

Red pine island.
Frosty mornings
    in the forest,
    in Kawishiwi country
        at Lake One.
Sparkling leaves.
Flashing gold and amber
    in afternoon sunshine
        along shorelines of tall pine
            and rugged outcroppings.

Red pine island.
Projecting perpetual green
    onto a landscape
    of changing colors
        and seasons transforming.
Blending into winter
    on chilly evening horizons
    of timelessness
        and time.

Fading away
    gently,
    relentlessly.

—October 2006 on solo canoe trip at Lake One

LONE MAPLE

Lone maple
   on Pauness shoreline,
   on rugged wilderness
      canvas—
Painted boldly
   with autumn colors
   and shades of seasons
      changing.

Brushstroke of red—
   burnt and blazing
   in stark contrast
      among aspen glow
      and evergreens.

Lone maple
   keeping lonely vigil
   on rocky shorelines
      shifting.
Changing in rhythms
   of passing life
   at ragged edges
      of reality.

Alone.
Like everyone—
   individual beauty
   standing out
      and blending in . . .

—December 2007 for Tom's autumn photograph taken years before at Pauness Lake

ISLE OF DREAMS

Sail away—
>> to sounds of solitude,
>> where imagination runs wild
>> and free.

Listen to hearts stirring,
>> rising within whispers
>> of new possibilities,
>> of hope on every horizon.

Travel—
>> to isle of dreams,
>> where creative spirits
>> seek renewal.

Sun shimmering on the water,
>> sinking behind towering pines
>> reaching higher,
>> deeper,
>> farther along the edges
>> of reality.

—August 1999 from a favorite little island in the middle of Lake Two

North of the Tension Line

NORTH OF THE TENSION LINE

Still
Small voice
    of calm,
    of comfort.

North of the tension line—

A refuge within:
    safe place,
    re-grouping space,
    peace in the midst
        of chaos.

A reservoir of strength:
    deep pool of courage
     to stand fast
        and stay grounded.

North of the tension line—

A place within where each day
    is a gift not a hassle,
        an opportunity
             not a problem,
        an invitation to discover
             new currents of life
                and laughter
                and love.

—August 1999 Northern Minnesota ambiance

PLACES OF THE HEART

North of ordinary—

An imaginary boundary
    dividing emotional reality
        into scenes
      of wonder
            and mystery.

South of contrary—

A fragmented edge
    crossing places of the heart
        with journeys
      of restless
            wandering.

—Undated and unknown context

DIAMOND HOUR

Diamond hour—
Sparkling
    through majestic branches
        teeming green
        with gentle leaves
            of life.

Shimmering
    from sunset skies
        dancing blue
        with heat waves
            of summer.

Sunshine melody
    breathing peacefulness
        into restless hearts
        at the dying of day
        and the birth
            of night.

Diamond hour—
    a precious gift
        of twilight relaxation,
    a beautiful treasure
        of meaningful connections,
        of the joy we share
           in our love
            for one another!

—*September 2000 for Norma and our back porch relaxation*

BLUE SHADOWS

Bright light.
Blue shadows.

Dim sun
        marches on
          through southern sky.

Winter afternoon beauty
        lingers long
        into twilight.

Bare branches.
Stark trees
        cast shadows
        on fallen snow.

Lovely hue.
Lonely
        and blue.

—December 2004 shadows on snow in our backyard woods

LONELY LOONS

Lonely loons
in a backwater bay.

Calling to no one—
    and everyone.

Piercing screams
    and haunting moans
        beckon all kindred spirits
            to a home
                away from home.

No longer strangers.
No need to roam.

—*September 1988 in the spirit of wildness*

ENDLESS ROCKS

Never enough
  rocks
  to find.

And gather.

Stones along the way—
  hunting treasures
  in old farm fields
      and along shorelines.
Throughout terrain
  scoured by ancient
      glaciers moving.

And melting.

Boulders lost in time
  coming alive
  in new walkways
      and along tree lines.

And in my heart.

—November 2007 picking rocks with Tom

STEAM RISING

Steam rising
  on calm birthday
      morning,
  on rugged shorelines
      icy.
And beautiful.

In ragged edges
  glistening like diamonds,
  sparkling in winter
      sunshine.
Blue shadows
  caressing frozen rocks
      and brightening snow,
  pointing places inland
      and far beyond.

Superior rising.

—*March 2008 for Norma's birthday at Cove Point Lodge on Lake Superior*

SOUL WHISPERS

Listening for whispers
   of the soul.

Difficult messages
   arriving through
        personal pain
        and sadness,
   seeping through
        all that is weary
        and wounded.

Deep in the soul.
Tough working
   on voices
        and visions.
Reflections of the heart
   weaving within
        multiple layers
        of confusion.
Accumulating
Piling up
   like autumn leaves.
Pressing down
   like fresh fallen snow
   long on the endless earth
        of time.

Soul whispers.

—November 2006 adaptation from "Soul Wrinkles"

SOUL WRINKLES

Ironing out
Wrinkles in the soul.

Difficult passages
    wading through
        personal pain
        and sadness,
    stretching through
        all that is weary
        and wounded.

Deep in the soul.
Tough working
    on rumples
    and wrinkles
Reflections of the heart
    weaving within
        multiple layers
        of clutter.

Accumulating
Piling up
    like yesterday's garbage.
Pressing down
    like smooth stones
    long in the endless river
        of time.

Soul wrinkles.

—September 2006 reflections of my heart while relaxing in the Boundary Waters Canoe Area Wilderness

About the Poet

I am a poet, pastor and longtime resident of Waconia—now working as a staff chaplain at Auburn Village in Chaska and Auburn Home in Waconia. My vision of chaplaincy ministry unfolds from a compassionate and joyful heart, and from twenty-nine years of experience serving as a congregational pastor and administrative leader. Trained by the Lombard Mennonite Peace Center, I also lead seminars on "Communication and Conflict For Changing Times." And for the past year I am enjoying monthly poetry reading gigs at the Mocha Monkey Coffee Shop in Waconia. With a folksy, multi-layered, down to earth, straightforward simplicity, I play with words, images and metaphors in poetic expressions of the experiences and relationships of life. All for the creative purpose of honestly making meanings and keeping memories alive. I have self-published two collections of poetry: *Isle Of Dreams* in 2002 and *Shades Of Gray* in 2005.